W9-CUN-873

The Berenstain Bears and the Nutcracker

Use your imagination!
Close your eyes and fly away
to the Nutcracker's magical kingdom
where sugar plum fairies play.

The Berenstain Bears® and the Nutcracker

Jan & Mike Berenstain

HARPER FESTIVAL

An Imprint of HarperCollinsPublishers

Copyright © 2011 by Berenstain Bears, Inc.

www.harpercollinschildrens.com
Library of Congress catalog card number: 2011924100
ISBN 978-0-06-057396-6

11 12 13 14 15   SCP   10 9 8 7 6 5 4 3 2 1
❖
First Edition

It was Christmas morning in Bear Country, and the sun was just beginning to peep through the window of the Bear family's tree house. Inside Papa was guarding the stairs while Mama switched on the Christmas tree lights.

"Okay," said Mama. "Turn 'em loose!"

Papa stood aside and Sister, Brother, and Honey dashed out to open their presents.

"Wow!" said Brother, opening a brightly wrapped package. "Look what Santa brought me—a brand-new video game, *Space Grizzlies*."

"And look what I got!" chimed in Sister. "A movie called *Bearbie's Amazing Adventure*! I can't wait to watch it."

"Look!" said Honey. "Look!"
    Her new toy was a battery-powered pony that could walk, whinny, and chew hay.

Happily the cubs opened the rest of the presents. The living room was soon filled with torn wrapping paper. Then Sister noticed an oddly shaped package behind the Christmas tree.

The label read, "For Brother, Sister, and Honey—from Santa." "This one is for all of us," Sister said.

Inside the package the cubs found a funny wooden soldier bear. He had a big mouth that opened and closed.

"What is this?" asked Sister.

"That's the Nutcracker Bear from *The Nutcracker* ballet," said Papa.

"Oh, yeah!" said Brother. "We saw that on TV."

The Nutcracker is about a young cub named Clara who gets a nutcracker for Christmas from her weird old godfather. She dreams the nutcracker comes to life and fights the Mouse King. He becomes a handsome prince and takes Clara to his magical kingdom, where they dance with snowflakes and the Sugar Plum Fairy. Clara wakes up and the prince turns back into a nutcracker.

"Does he crack nuts?" asked Brother, trying the nutcracker out. They cracked some walnuts in his jaws. He worked just fine.

"Great," said Brother, munching on walnuts, "but I want to play with my other presents."

"Me, too!" said Sister.

"Too!" said Honey.

The cubs got busy with their brand-new toys, games, and videos.

By early afternoon, something odd happened. The cubs were tired of their new things. Brother played video games until his eyes were about to fall out. Sister watched her Bearbie movie over and over until she couldn't stand the sight of pink.

N-E-E-I-G-H!

Honey played with her battery-operated pony so much that it finally broke.

"We're bored!" Sister complained to Mama and Papa.

"But you have all these new presents to play with," said Mama.

"I know," said Brother. "But we're bored anyway."

"Well, you'll have to figure out something to do until company comes for Christmas dinner," said Mama.

"Why don't you use your imaginations?" said Papa.

"Our imaginations?" said Sister. "How do we do that?"

"You just pretend," said Papa. "Go up to the attic and make yourselves costumes out of old clothes and pretend something."

"Like what?" asked Brother.

"Anything," said Papa. "Pirates or space grizzlies or cowbears or bears-in-armor or—"

"Or the nutcracker!" said Sister, picking up the Nutcracker Bear.

"Yeah!" said Brother. "We could fight those giant mice!"

"Yeah!" said Honey.

So the cubs took the nutcracker up the creaky stairs to the attic.

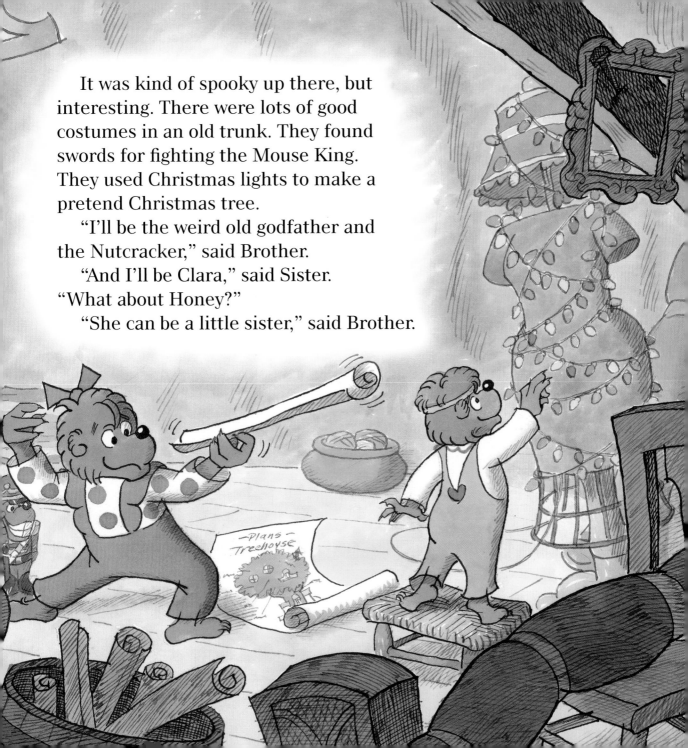

It was kind of spooky up there, but interesting. There were lots of good costumes in an old trunk. They found swords for fighting the Mouse King. They used Christmas lights to make a pretend Christmas tree.

"I'll be the weird old godfather and the Nutcracker," said Brother.

"And I'll be Clara," said Sister. "What about Honey?"

"She can be a little sister," said Brother.

The cubs put on their costumes and used their imaginations.

"Merry Christmas, Clara!" said her godfather. "Here is your present, a Nutcracker Bear."

"Oh, thank you, dear Godfather!" said Clara. "I love him—he's so cute!"

But the little sister grabbed the nutcracker and broke it.

"Hey!" said Clara. "Stop that!"

"Here you are," said her godfather, giving the nutcracker back. "I fixed it so it's as good as new. Now it's time to go to bed."

The cubs pretended to go to bed. Then the clock began to strike midnight.

"What's happening?" said Clara.

Her godfather was up on the clock, and the Christmas tree was growing! The attic seemed to be turning into the world of *The Nutcracker*.

"Oh, no!" said Clara.
"The Mouse King is attacking!

"Hooray!" she cried. "It's my nutcracker! He's come to life. He will save us!"

"Oh, dear!" Clara said. "The Mouse King is winning! What can I do?

"I know! I'll throw my slipper at him!" she decided.

"My brave nutcracker!" said Clara. "But, wait!
Now you look like a handsome prince!"

"Yes," the Nutcracker said. "The spell that made me
into a nutcracker is broken. Now let's fly away to my
magical kingdom!"

"Okay!" said Clara.

Off they flew through the night.

"Here we are in the Land of Snow," said the prince. "See the dancing snowflakes?"

"Aren't they lovely!" said Clara. "*Brrr! It's cold!*"

They flew on.

"Welcome to the Land of Sweets," said the prince.

"It looks delicious," said Clara.

"Let's dance!" said the prince.

"Okay!" said Clara.

"Sister! Brother! Honey!" called a voice.

"Time for dinner!" called
Mama from downstairs.
"Okay, Mama," answered
the cubs.
The world of *The Nutcracker*
seemed to fade away. They put
away their costumes and brought
the nutcracker down from the attic.

Grizzly Gramps and Gran were there for Christmas dinner.

"A Nutcracker Bear!" said Grizzly Gran, "How cute! Do you cubs know the story of *The Nutcracker*?"

"We sure do!" said Brother. "We'll act it out for you."

"Are you going to put on the whole Nutcracker ballet without costumes or sets or anything?" asked Grizzly Gramps.

"That's right, Gramps," said Sister. "You just have to use your imagination."

And that's exactly what they did!